El León y el Ratón
Una Fábula de Esopo

The Lion and the Mouse
an Aesop's Fable

Jan Ormerod

Spanish translation by Marta Belen Saez-Cabero

Hace mucho tiempo en un lejano país, un pequeño ratón trepó por la cola de un león mientras este dormía. Subió corriendo por su lomo y su melena hasta llegar a la cabeza ...

... y acabó despertando al león.

Far away and long ago, as a lion lay asleep, a little mouse ran up his tail. He ran onto his back and up his mane and onto his head ...

... so that the lion woke up.

El león atrapó al ratón y, sujetándolo con sus grandes garras, rugió enojado: "¡Cómo te atreves a despertarme! ¿Acaso no sabes que soy el Rey de las Bestias? ¡Y te comeré!"

The lion grabbed the mouse and, holding him in his large claws, roared in anger: "How dare you wake me up! Don't you know that I am the King of the Beasts? And I shall eat you!"

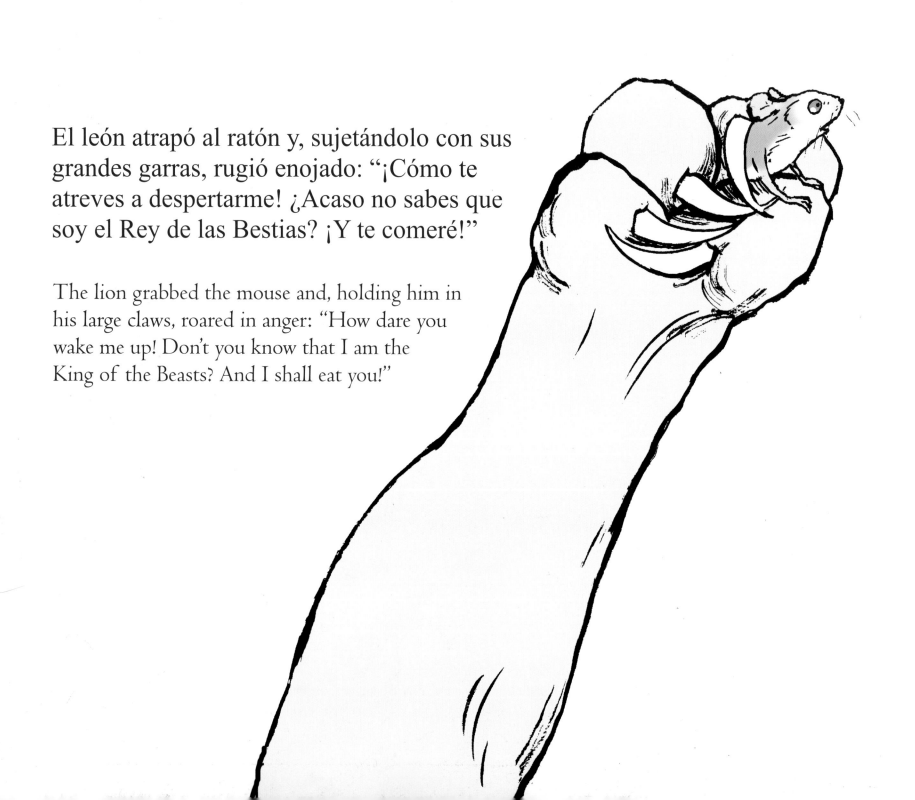

El ratón suplicó al león que lo soltara. "¡Por favor, Majestad, no me coma! Por favor, suélteme y le prometo que seré su amigo para siempre. Quién sabe, quizás un día hasta le salve la vida".

The mouse begged the lion to let him go. "Please don't eat me Your Majesty! Please let me go - and I promise I will be your friend forever. Who knows, one day I might even save your life."

El león miró al ratoncito y soltó una risotada. "¿Que *tú* vas a salvar *mi* vida?
¡Qué tontería! Pero me has hecho reír y me has puesto de buen humor.
Así que dejaré que te vayas".
Y el león abrió sus garras para liberar al ratón.

The lion looked at the tiny mouse and burst out laughing. "*You* save *my* life?
What a silly idea! But you have made me laugh and put me into a good mood.
So I shall let you go."
And the lion opened his claws and set the mouse free.

Pocos días después el león quedó atrapado en la red de un cazador. A pesar de su tamaño y de su fuerza no podía liberarse. Lanzó un rugido de rabia que hizo temblar la tierra.

It was only a few days later that the lion was trapped by a hunter's net.
Even with all his size and strength he could not break free.
He let out a roar of rage that shook the earth.

Todos los animales oyeron su grito …

All the animals heard his cry ...

pero sólo el ratoncito salió corriendo en la dirección del rugido del león. "Yo le ayudaré, Majestad", dijo el ratón. "Usted me liberó y no me comió. Así que ahora soy su amigo y siervo de por vida".

but only the tiny mouse ran in the direction of the lion's roar. "I will help you, Your Majesty," said the mouse. "You let me go and did not eat me. So now I am your friend and helper for life."

Inmediatamente se puso a roer las cuerdas que ataban al león.

He immediately began gnawing at the ropes that bound the lion.

El ratoncito mordisqueó hasta que se puso el sol.
Royó mientras la luna y las estrellas aparecían en
el cielo. Por fin, justo antes del amanecer, el Rey
de las Bestias quedó libre.

The tiny mouse nibbled until the sun went down.
He gnawed as the moon and stars appeared in the sky.
Finally, just before the sun rose again,
the King of the Beasts was free at last.

"¿A que tenía razón, Majestad?", dijo el pequeño ratón.
"Me tocaba ayudarle".
Entonces el león no se rio del ratoncito, sino que dijo:
"No creía que me pudieras ser útil, ratoncito, pero hoy
me has salvado la vida".

"Was I not right, Your Majesty?" said the little mouse.
"It was my turn to help you."
The lion did not laugh at the little mouse now,
but said, "I did not believe that you could be
of use to me, little mouse, but today
you saved my life."

Teacher's Notes

The Lion and the Mouse

Read the story. Explain that we can write our own fable by changing the characters.

Discuss the different animals you could use, for instance would a dog rescue a cat? What kind of situation could they be in that a dog might rescue a cat?

Write an example together as a class, then, give the children the opportunity to write their own fable. Children who need support could be provided with a writing frame.

As a whole class play a clapping, rhythm game on various words in the text working out how many syllables they have.

Get the children to imagine that they are the lion. They are so happy that the mouse rescued them that they want to have a party to say thank you. Who would they invite? What kind of food might they serve? Get the children to draw the different foods or if they are older to plan their own menu.

The Hare's Revenge

Many countries have versions of this story including India, Tibet and Sri Lanka. Look at a map and show the children the countries.

Look at the pictures with the children and compare the countries that the lions live in – one is an arid desert area and the other is the lush green countryside of Malaysia.

Children can write their own fables by changing the setting of this story. Think about what kinds of animals you would find in a different setting. For example, how about 'The Hedgehog's Revenge', starring a hedgehog and a fox, living near a farm.

The hare thinks the lion is a bully and that he always gets others to do things for him. Discuss with the children different ways that the lion could be stopped from bullying. The children could role play different ways of dealing with the bullying lion.

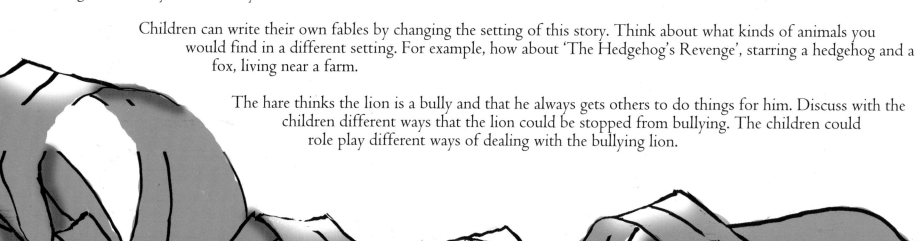

La Venganza de la Liebre
Una Fábula Malasia

The Hare's Revenge
A Malaysian Fable

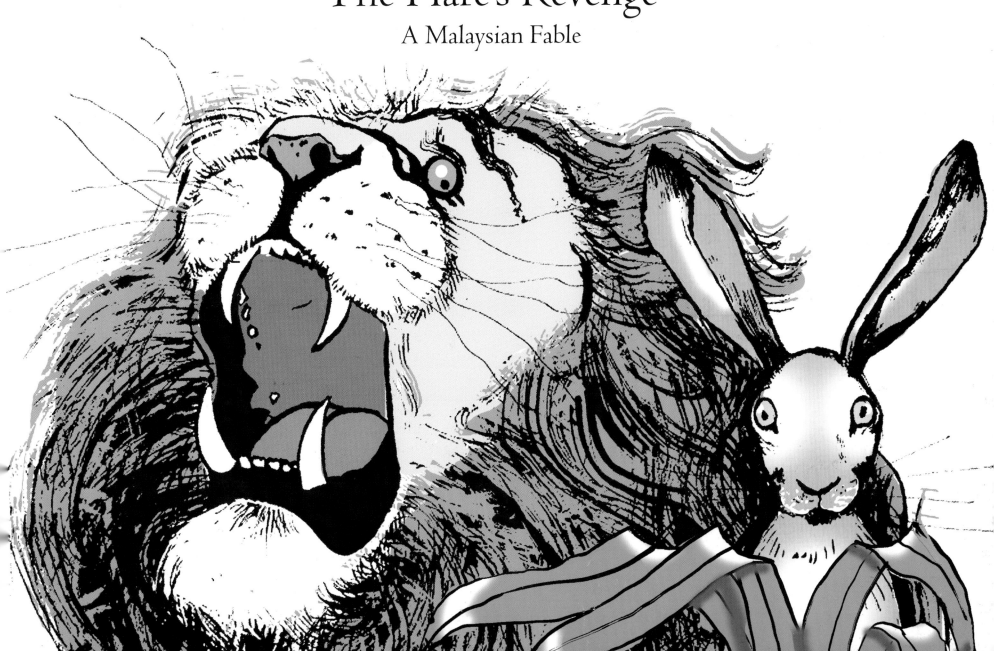

Una liebre y un león eran vecinos.

"Soy el Rey de los Bosques", presumía el león. "Soy fuerte y valiente y nadie puede retarme".

"Sí, Majestad", respondía la liebre con una voz débil y asustadiza. Entonces el león rugía hasta lastimar las orejas de la liebre, y bramaba hasta poner a la liebre muy triste.

A hare and a lion were neighbours.

"I am the King of the Woods," the lion would boast. "I am strong and brave and no one can challenge me."

"Yes Your Majesty," the hare would reply in a small, frightened voice. Then the lion would roar until the hare's ears hurt, and he would rage until the hare felt very unhappy.

Finalmente, la liebre pensó: "¡Ya estoy harta! Esc león es un matón y un tonto y debo vengarme".
Así que se acercó al león y le dijo: "Buen día, Majestad. He conocido a un león que es igualito a usted. Este león me dijo que ÉL era el rey de estos bosques, y que se libraría de cualquiera que le retase".

Finally, the hare thought, "I can stand it no longer.
That lion is a bully and a fool and I must get my revenge."
So, she went to the lion and said, "Good day,
Your Majesty. I've met a lion who looks
exactly like you. This lion said HE
was the king of these woods and
that he would see off anyone
who challenged him."

"¡Cómo!", dijo el león. "¿Y no le hablaste de *mí*?"
"Sí, lo hice", contestó la liebre. "Pero habría sido mejor si no lo
hubiera hecho. Cuando le describí lo fuerte que sois, se mofó.
Y dijo unas cosas muy groseras. ¡Incluso dijo que no le
serviríais ni como criado!"

"Oho," the lion said. "Didn't you mention *me* to him?"
"Yes, I did," the hare replied. "But it would have been better if I
hadn't. When I described how strong you were, he just sneered.
And he said some very rude things. He even said
that he wouldn't take *you* for his servant!"

El león montó en cólera. "¿Dónde está? ¿Dónde está? Como encuentre a ese león", rugió, "ya le enseñaré quién es el Rey de estos Bosques".
"Si así lo desea Su Majestad", respondió la liebre, "puedo llevarle a su escondrijo".

The lion flew into a rage. "Where is he? Where is he? If I could find that lion,"
he roared, "I would soon teach him who is King of these Woods."
"If Your Majesty would like," answered the hare, "I could take you to his hiding place."

Así que la liebre llevó al león a un pozo
profundo y dijo: "Está ahí abajo".

So the hare took the lion to a deep well and said, "He is down there."

El león miró enfurecido dentro del pozo. Allí estaba
un león enorme y feroz, mirándole a él con odio.
El león rugió, y un rugido todavía más fuerte resonó
en el interior del pozo.

The lion glared angrily into the well.
There, was a huge ferocious lion, glaring back at him.
The lion roared, and an even louder roar echoed up
from within the well.

Lleno de rabia el león pegó un salto y se arrojó sobre el feroz león del pozo.

Filled with rage the lion sprang into the air and flung himself at the ferocious lion in the well.

Cayó y
 cayó y
  cayó y
   nunca más se le volvió a ver.

Down and
 down and
  down he fell
   never to be seen again.

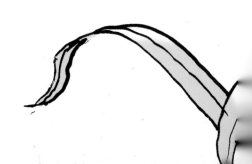

Y así es como la liebre se vengó.

And that was how the hare had her revenge.